Richard Scarry's
PIG WILL
and
PIG WON'T
A BOOK OF MANNERS

Random House New York

The Pig Family

Mother Pig and Daddy Pig have two little pigs—
Pig Will and Pig Won't.
Whenever they are asked to do something,
Pig Will says, "I will."
But Pig Won't always says, "I won't."

If Mother Pig asks them to please be quiet,
Pig Will whispers, "I will."
Pig Won't shouts out, "I WON'T!" Bad boy!

At breakfast Daddy Pig tells them to eat like good little pigs.
Pig Will uses a fork and takes small bites.
Pig Won't likes to talk with his mouth full.
Doesn't he have awful manners!

Pig Will helps clear
the table.
Pig Won't won't.

When Daddy Pig washes the dishes,
Pig Will always dries them.
Pig Won't never does. He is no help at all.

If Mother Pig asks,
"Who will water my flower garden?"
Pig Will says, "I will."
Pig Won't says, "I won't."
He waters a lady's hat instead.
Stop that, Pig Won't!

When they are told to go to bed,
Pig Will runs straight off to bed.
Pig Won't won't.

For being a bad, disobedient pig,
Pig Won't gets a spanking
from his daddy.
Will that teach him to behave,
I wonder?

Going Shopping

One day Mother Pig asks,
"Who will help me do my shopping?"
Pig Won't says he would rather stay in bed.
"Very well," says Mother Pig.
"Pig Will and I are going without you."

Mother Pig and Pig Will
drive off to the supermarket.

The supermarket is having a special fair today.
Pig Will is given a red balloon.
He is also given an ice cream cone.

Pig Will has a ride
on a pony.

Then Pig Will has a ride in an airplane.
He is having lots of fun.

Now it is time to do the shopping.
Mother Pig buys all her groceries.
She lets Pig Will buy a package of seeds for planting.

Mr. Frumble is shopping too.
Mr. Frumble always makes trouble.
Uh-oh! Watch out, everybody!

Meanwhile, Pig Won't gets up.
He wants Daddy Pig to take him to the playground.
But Daddy is busy working. He has no time for Pig Won't.

Pig Won't goes to the kitchen.
He can't find any cookies, so
he decides he won't have breakfast.

He turns on the television,
but he can't make it work.

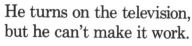

He won't learn to read,
so he can't read a book.

Pig Won't has nothing to do.
"Come play with me," he says to Bunny.
"No," Bunny answers. "I am going
shopping with my daddy."

On the way home Mother Pig and Pig Will
stop at an ice cream parlor
and have ice cream sodas.

When they arrive home, Pig Won't is hungry and crying.
When he hears about all the fun Pig Will had,
he cries even harder. I can't feel sorry for you, Pig Won't.

Corn on the Cob

Pig Will is ready to plant his package of seeds.
"Will you help me?" he asks his brother.
"No, I won't," Pig Won't answers.
Lowly Worm, who is passing by, says, "I will."

So Lowly and Pig Will dig holes for the seeds.

One day Pig Will asks,
"Will you help me water the plants?"
"No, I won't," says Pig Won't.
"Then Lowly and I will water
the plants," says Pig Will.
And that's just what they do.

The corn grows and grows.
At last it is ready to be picked.
"Will you help us now?" asks Pig Will.
"Of course I won't!" says Pig Won't.
"Then Lowly and I will do it
all by ourselves," says Pig Will.
And that's just what they do.

When Lowly and Pig Will finish picking the corn,
they bring it to Mother Pig.

Mother Pig cooks it for them.
"Who is going to eat this delicious corn?" she asks.
"I will," says Pig Will.
"I will," says Lowly Worm.
"Me too!" says Pig Won't.

"Oh no, you won't!" shouts Pig Will.
"You wouldn't help plant the corn.
You wouldn't help water the corn.
You wouldn't help pick the corn.
And you won't help eat it!"

Pig Won't loves corn.
And now he has to watch Pig Will and
Lowly eat it all up.
Too bad! But it serves you right, Pig Won't.
If you don't do your share of the work,
you don't deserve a share of the rewards.

Guess Who?

Guess who plays nicely with other children
and shares his toys?
That's easy, right? It's Pig Will!

When Mother Pig asks him to stop rocking
in his chair, this little pig keeps doing it anyway.

Oops! See what happens, Pig Won't,
when you don't listen!

Who is always teasing younger children?
Will you stop that, Pig Won't!
But do you think he will?

The Birthday Party

Tomorrow is Pig Will's birthday.
Mother Pig is busy getting ready for the party.

"Why don't you boys go out to play," she says.
"It looks like it may rain, so you must
put on your raincoats and hats and boots.
You don't want to get sick for the party."

Pig Won't hates to wear a raincoat and boots.
As soon as he is outside, he takes them off.
Naughty pig!

Soon it begins to rain.
Pig Won't gets soaking wet.

To make matters worse
he climbs a tree and—

—falls off.
He lands in a mud puddle.
See! Mother Pig told you not to climb trees
until you are older.

When they come home,
Mother Pig is furious at Pig Won't.
She dries him off and then everybody has lunch.

After they eat, Mother Pig asks,
"Who will help clear the table?"
"I will," says Pig Will.
"AAAHCHOOO!" sneezes Pig Won't.
He has caught a cold because he
didn't mind his mother.

Mother Pig sends him straight to bed.
"Take this medicine right now," she says.

The next day all the children
arrive for Pig Will's party.

Pig Won't hears all the fun,
but he can't join them.
He is very sad.

Although Pig Won't doesn't deserve it,
Lowly Worm brings him a piece
of birthday cake to go with his cough medicine.
"It's too bad you couldn't have been
at the party," says Lowly.
That's what sometimes happens to naughty pigs.

Pig Won't's Decision

The next day Pig Won't is better.
"That was very nice of you, Lowly,
to bring me the cake," says Pig Won't.
"It's nice to be nice," Lowly tells him.
"You should try it sometimes.
Then you will have many friends."
Pig Won't thinks about that.

Please
Please
Please
Please

And from that day on,
Pig Won't decides that
he will try to be good.
He always says "please"
when he asks
for something.

Thank you
Thank you
Thank you

urrnkyuu

He always says "thank you"
when someone gives him something.

When his mother asks, "Who will take out the garbage?"
"I will," says Pig Will.
"Me too," says Pig Won't.

"Who will help me with the dishes?" asks Daddy Pig.
"I will," says Pig Will.
"Me too," says Pig Won't.

"Who will help me do my shopping?" asks Mother Pig.
"I will," says Pig Will.
"Me too," says Pig Won't.

He plays nicely with other children
and has made many friends.

He always does as he is told.
"Yes, Mother," he says.

And when Mother Pig asks,
"Who will give me
a big hug and kiss?"
Pig Will says, "I will."
And Pig Won't says, "Me too."

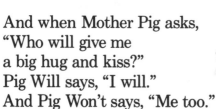

And do you know what? He isn't Pig Won't anymore.
He's Pig Me Too. And everybody likes him.